Nokum
IS MY TEACHER

BY **David Bouchard** ~ PAINTINGS BY **Allen Sapp**
SINGING AND DRUMMING BY **Northern Cree**

Red Deer PRESS

Will you walk with me, Grandmother?
Will you talk with me a while?
I'm finding life confusing
And I'm looking for some answers
To questions all around me
At that school and on the street.
You have always been here for me.
Will you help me learn to see?

Aren't there others, boy, around you
Who know little more than you?
Others older but not wiser
Who have yet to understand?

Kâ-kîwici pimôhtêmin ci nôhkom?
Kâ-kîwici pikiskwâtitin ci aciyow?
Mitoni ôma ê-pikwêtamân.
Anite kiskinohamâtokamikohk êkwa mîna
   mêskanak.
Kâkike ê-kîwicihin.
Kâki ci êkwa kiskinohamowin?

Kotakahk ci kâ-kikwêcimawak nosim,
Ekiskêtakik ayiwak ispici kiya?
Kotakahk ayiwâk e-kitêyicik, kiyâpic ayiwâk
   mâka kânistotakik.

Would you answer something simple?
Help me see just what they want.
I can't help but think and wonder,
There is so much to be learned.
I can't help but look and wonder.
I get lost at every turn.

Are the answers in the oak tree
Or the wispy, tender birch?
Do you know what I am asking?
Will you please answer this first?

Should the answer to some questions
Not be sought within your heart?

Kâ-kiwitamôwin ci kikway?
Ka-wihcihin tawâpâhtamân kikway
  entawîtakik?
Mitoni nipikwêtin,
Iko mistahi kakiskêtaman.
Niwanihison.

Mitosak ci nakiwitamâkohk?
Kikiskêtin ci kikwây ekwecikêmoyan?
Ka-kîwihtamowin ci oma?

Kitehik anima kamiskên kikwây
Anima kantoniman.

Just one thing then, my Nokum
Just a simple answer, please!
Do you think the white world's meant for me?
You know how hard that life can be.

And do they even know or care
That we are here, that we were there?
Do you think they care at all
About *our* ways, about *our* culture?

Have you yet to find another
Who is fit to judge your heart?

Peyak kikway maka nohkom,
Moniyânâhk ci naki-pimâtisin?
Ki-kiskêyitin îko ê-âyimak êkwanima
   pimâtisowin.

Namakîkway nakatôkewak ota e-hayâyak.
Kiteyitin ci enâkatôkêcik nehiyaw
   pimâtisowin?

Kimiskawaw ci âwiyak,
Ka-wesiwatak kiteh?

Answer this then please, Grandmother,
Why must I go to their school?
I am told to sit and listen,
I'm supposed to somehow care
About their towns and their big cities,
Their fast cars and pretty things.
If they ever stopped to ask me
I'd prefer to drum and sing.

Can the reason they don't understand
Not somehow lie in your small hands?

Naskômin mâka nohkom?
Tanihki mâka êkotê kanitaw
   kiskinohamâkosiyân?
E-witamâkoyiyan ka-apiyân ekwa
   ka-nitôhtamân.
Kakwe nâkatôkeyan ocenâsihk,
   sohkepimpâyisak êkwa
Ka-miyosikik kîkway.
Kîspin kakwêcimikowiyân, nawache piko
   nanohtê nikamon.

Apwêtikwê namoya ekiskîtakik
 Êkota eyasteki kichichisa.

The teacher at that school today
Said reading would help set me free.
She told me that her books were key
To understanding nature, yet
She's never walked a snowy path
In darkness on a starlit night.
She's never met a hungry wolf
Alone without a soul in sight.

Had you, my child, not learned to read,
How would you see the broken reed
That tells of rabbit, fox, or deer
Or that lone wolf you've seen so near?

Kiskinohamâkew anita
    kiskinohamâtokamikohk,
Êkîwitamowit kîspin ka-âyamicikeyân,
Wâyiyow natotayikon.
Ekîwitamowit masinahikanak apîkwekana
Kanistotaman pimâtisowin.
Êkwa namoya wîkâc wiya epimohtêt
Kona meskanâk kâ-tipiskak.
Namoya nakiskâwew mahikana e-pêyikot.

Apo ci nitawâsimis, kispin namôya
    ki-âyamicikan,
Namoya kanistotin pimâtisowin ka-witak
    wâpos,
Mahkêsis, âpo apsimosis êkota e-kiyayât.

That's not the kind of reading
That we do inside that school.
The books they have are of *their* world,
They don't play by our people's rules.

And is it not the Maker's way
To have the strong survive?
Please tell me true, my Nokum,
Spare nothing, tell no lies.

Do we want our children's stories
To remember us this way:
As people just too proud to learn
From things we see at every turn?

Namoya anima kiyânaw peyakwan
Ka-ayamicikiyâk ekota
  kiskinohamâtokamikohk.
Masinahikanak anihi ka-ayâcik,
Namoya anima kiyânaw kipimâtisinânaw.

Kisêmanito anihi wichihêw ka-maskosicik.
Wihtamowin nôhkom, kaya kiyâskimin.

Ekosi ci kitawasimisinâwak
  kisimâmtonayimkoyakik?
Apo ci kiyanaw îko e-kicemisoyahk
Kakisketamak kotahk pimâtisowin?

I love the way *you* teach me
Through stories and through songs.
Through drumming and through singing
We have learned this way so long.

I love the way *you* teach me
Through your stories and your songs.
I don't need books to learn, do I?
Please tell me, am I wrong?

Do you know how I would feel today
If I could share my love this way?
My heart and soul I'd write for you
That you might read and share yours too.

Nisâhkitan oma kikway kakiskinohâmowin.
Acimowina ekwa nikamowina e-âpacitayin.
Kayas ohci ekiskitamak.

Nisâhkitan oma kikway kakiskinohâmowin,
Acimowina ekwa nikamowina.
Namoya kakatâc mashinahikanak
    ka-âpacitayan ci?
Witamowin kispin namoya kwêsk
    e-mamtoniyitamân?

Kikisketin ci tanisi ki-tamâcohiyan
Kispin awiyak kasâkihak?
Namasinahin oma nitêh ekwa nitâchâk
Kista ka-âyamitayin.

If these things are important,
Why did *you* not learn to read?
Or Mosom or my uncles?
They must not have seen a need.

We've lived out here for years this way
Without the things *they* say we need.
If these things are important
Why did *you* not learn to read?

Would you ask all these questions
Had I learned to read when I was young?
Do you think you'd be so troubled
Had your Nokum read when she was young?

Kispin e-wîchasik, tanihki mâka kiya
Namoya eki-âyamicikiyin, âpo nimosom
   ekwa nohcâwisak?
Namoya ewichasik teyitamohk.

Kinwes ota ki-wîkinaw.
Namoya kâ-katac ekosisi kitwêcik ka
   pimâtisoyahk.
Kispin iko ê-wichasik, tanihki mâka kiya
   epe-âyamicikêyin?

Kakwecikemowin ci kâpêkiskiyitaman,
Ka-âyamicikiyan ê-oskayawiyan?
Kîspin kohkom âyamicikêw e-oskyahot,
Kîteyitin ci anohc mistahi kawâniyitin?

I'd never blame you, Grandma.
You are everything I want to be.
I'd never blame you, Nokum.
You know how much you mean to me.

Yet, you told me that all things must
        change,
That no one is exempt.
Please tell me as my teacher,
Is this not just what you meant?

It might be time for you
To answer me a simple thing:
Is truth not what you seek today
By hearing what I have to say?

Namoya wikâc katâmîyimitin nôhkom.
Nitawîyitin peyakwan kâ-âyisiniwiyan.
Namoya wikâc katâmîyimitin nohkom.
Kikiskiyitin tanimâyikohk ê-sakihitân.

Ê-kiwitamowiyin kâkiyaw kikwây pitos
        e-wisipayik.
Namawiyak pîtos.
Witamowin, kiya ôma kâ-kiskina-
        hamôwiyin,
Ekosi ci ôma êyaspayik?

Apwetikwe takinaskotamâwiyin kikway:
Anohc ci oma ka-nososâkaman tâpwewin
Kapetamân kikwaya ê-itwêyin?

You've taught me everything I know,
To walk and talk—to sing and drum,
To know the tree deserves respect
To feel, to care, to love and yet . . .

You know my heart, grandmother,
As you know the track of deer.
But why must we fit in their world?
Our lives are fine out here!

Are we not all the children
Of the one great Manito?

Should we not share our learnings?
Is that not what he would do?

Piko kikway kâkiskitamân
    ê-kiskinohamôwihin,
Ka-pimohtêyân, ka-pikiskwêyân,
    ka-nikamoyân,
Êkwa ka- pahkamahak mistikwaskîhk.
Ka-kiskitamân mîtos kâ-sahkihit.
Kosi ecikôma e-yisayâk ka-sâhkitayan
    kîkway.
Nitêh kikiskiyitin nôhkom,
Tanîhki ôma êkote ênohte pimâtisiyak?
Asay kiyânaw ôte ê-pimatisiyak.

Namoya ci kiyânaw manito awâsisak?
Namoya ci kotâwinaw kitiyitam?
Kakikisikinomâkiyak ci kikway
    e-kiskiyitamak?
Ekosi ci manito kîtotam?

I know you're right and I *will* read.
I now have come to see a need.
I'll use it as we use our songs
And hope it serves us just as long.

I think I've found the answer,
And with little help from you.
You haven't answered anything.
You've made *me* answer everything!

I'm waiting, child, to lend a hand
When I know that you need me.
For now your Nokum is content
To watch you learn to see.

Nikiskîyiten ê-tâpweyin êkwa nika
   âyamicikan.
Niwâpatin êkwa tânihki.
Nitâpacitân peyakwan kâ-âpacitayân
   nikamowina.
Kinwês ka-âpacitânaw.

Nimâmitonîyitin êkwa namoya
   ê-wichihiyin.
Namoya ki wihtamôwin, kahkiyaw
   niskwêyitin.

Ê-pewiyan ôma nôsim,
Tansisi kisiswîchitan?
Ê-kiskitamân piko tawîchitan.
Tepehiten êkwa kohkom,
Kiskiyitamowin ka-wahpatên.

Northern Lights Books for Children published by
Red Deer Press
A Fitzhenry & Whiteside Company
1512, 1800–4 Street S.W.
Calgary, Alberta, Canada T2S 2S5
www.reddeerpress.com

Credits
Edited for the Press by Dennis Johnson
Copyedited by Kirstin Morrell
Cree translation by Steve Wood
Recorded by Bruce Cutknife
Mastered by Geoff Edwards
Cover and text design by Erin Woodward
Printed and bound in China by Paramount Book Art for Red Deer Press

Acknowledgments
Financial support provided by the Canada Council, and the Government of Canada through the Book Publishing Industry Development Program (BPIDP).

National Library of Canada Cataloguing in Publication
Bouchard, Dave, 1952-
Nokum is my teacher / David Bouchard; Allen Sapp, illustrator; music by Northern Cree.
Text in English and Cree. Accompanied by a CD.
ISBN 0-88995-367-8
I. Sapp, Allen, 1929- II. Northern Cree Singers. III. Title.
PS8553.O759N65 2006   jC811'.54   C2006-904648-4

Nokum – I dedicate this book to you. It has taken me some time, but I have finally learned (initially from an Odawa Elder) that so much of what I am has come to me through my DNA, through my genes…through memories that I have inherited from you. I recognize your presence and I celebrate our family's collective memories. Nokum, I know now that YOU are my teacher. My successes are OUR successes. Marcee…